A gift from Egmont

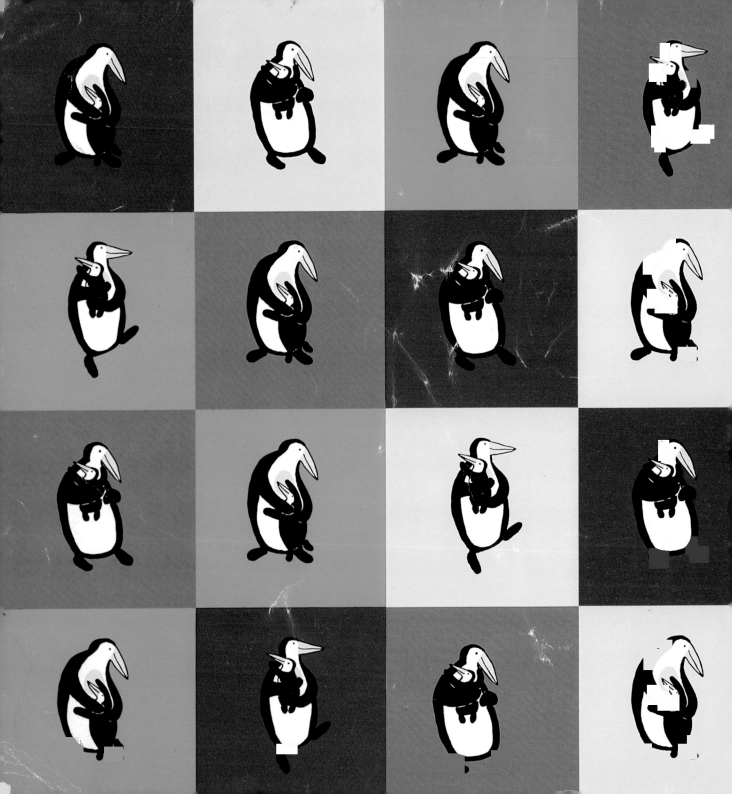

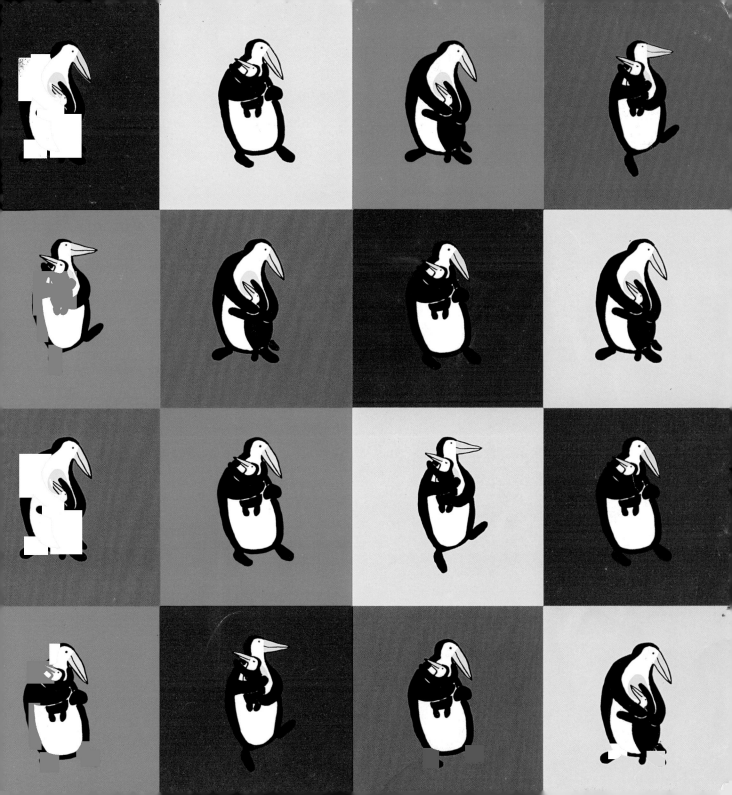

To Brian

On behalf of Bookstart, Egmont would like to thank:
Mary Murphy, for kindly agreeing to waive her royalties;
Anglia Graphics, for providing their services for free;
and Oriental Press Limited,who have made
an invaluable contribution by generously
discounting the printing costs of the books.

First published in Great Britain in 1997
by Methuen Children's Books
an imprint of Egmont Books Limited
239 Kensington High Street, London W8 6SA
This edition especially produced for Bookstart
in Great Britain in 2001 by Egmont Books Limited
Copyright © Mary Murphy 1997
Mary Murphy has asserted her moral rights

ISBN 0 7497 4926 1

1 3 5 7 9 10 8 6 4 2

Printed and bound in UAE by Oriental Press

I like it when......

Mary Murphy

EGMONT

I like it

when

you

hold

my

hand

I like it

when

you

let

me

help

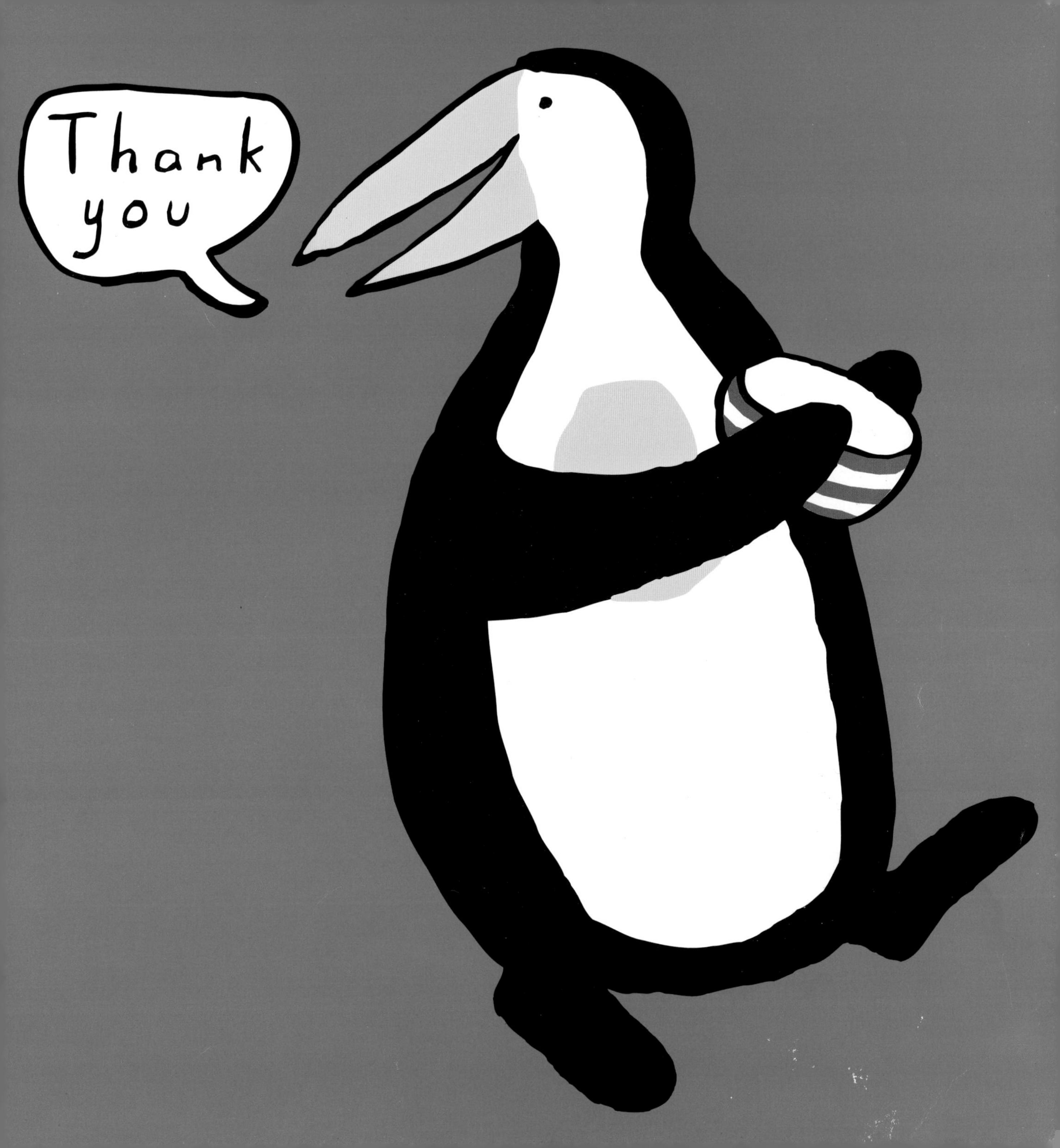
Thank you

I like it when we

I like it when we

play peekaboo

I like it when you tickle me

I like it when

you dance with me

I like it
when
you
read
me
stories

I like it when

you hug me tight

I like it when we
splash about

I like it
when
we
kiss
goodnight

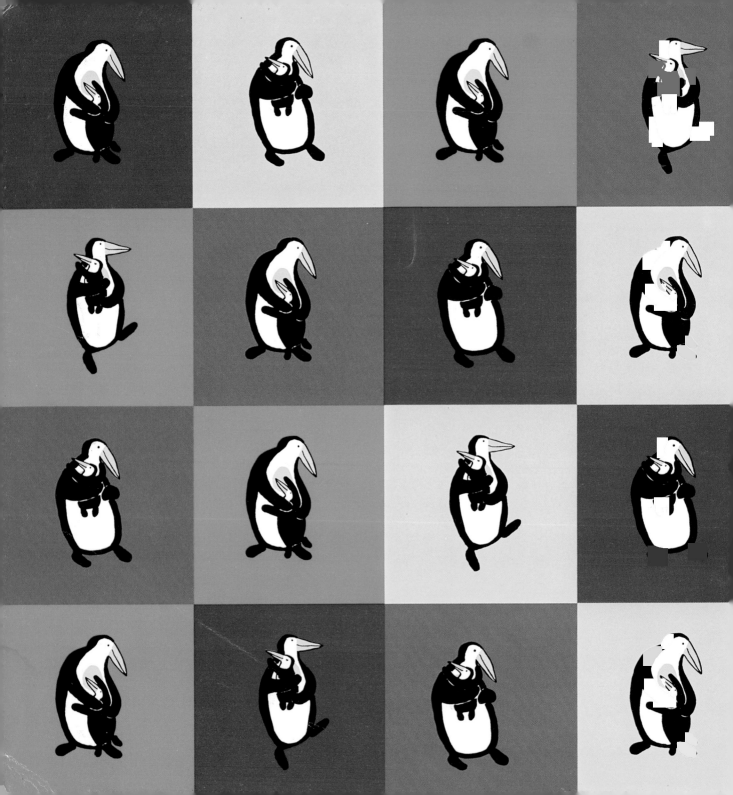

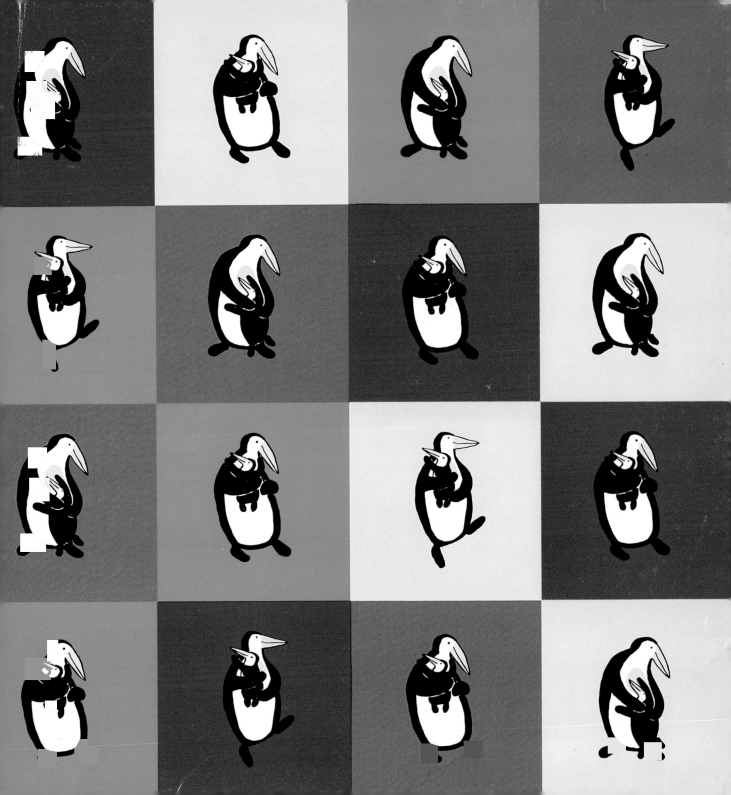

There are lots more stories from Mary Murphy for you to enjoy:

ISBN 0 7497 4212 7

ISBN 0 7497 3651 8

ISBN 0 7497 3241 5

ISBN 0 7497 3920 7

ISBN 0 7497 3919 3

ISBN 0 7497 3870 7

ISBN 0 7497 3869 3

ISBN 0 7497 4407 3